# Do MonKeys Tweet?

# Dedicated to Nigel, Ben and George

For information about this and other Houghton Mifflin trade and reference books
and multimedia products, visit The Bookstore at Houghton Mifflin
on the World Wide Web at http://www.hmco.com/trade/.

Manufactured in China

10 9 8 7 6 5 4 3 2 1

Library of Congress Cataloging–in–Publication Data
Walsh, Melanie.
Do monkeys tweet? / by Melanie Walsh. — 1st American ed.
p.    cm.
Summary: Asks such questions as "Do little mice purr?" and
"Do butterflies growl?" and then tells which animal makes each specific sound.
ISBN 0–395–85081–9
1. Animal sounds–Juvenile literature. [1. Animal sounds.]
I. Title.
QL765.W35      1997
591.59-dc20     96-35111
CIP
AC

# Do Monkeys Tweet?

# Melanie Walsh

Houghton Mifflin Company

Boston 1997

Do
horses
bark?

Do little
mice purr?

No, cats purr.

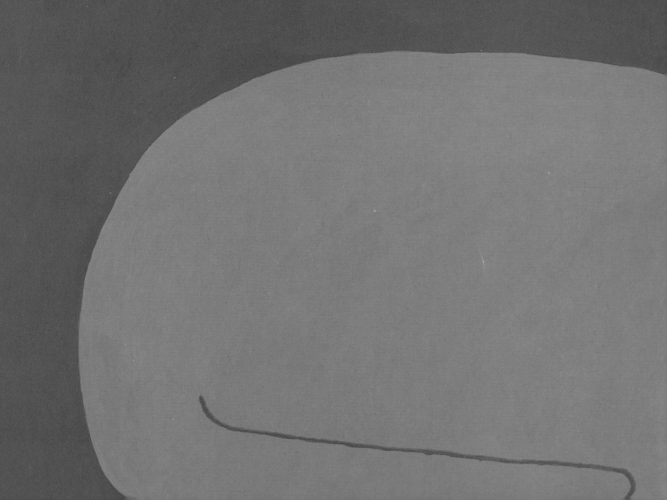

# Do baby lambs go

**buzz?**

No, bees go buzz.

# Do camels cheep?

cheep

# No, chicks
# cheep !

cheep

cheep

cheep

cheep

Do butterflies growl?

No, but
tigers do!

grrrr

# Do rabbits go oink?

oink oink

No, pigs go oink !

Do owls
go hoot in
the middle of
the night?

Yes they do!